P9-CTQ-312

THIS BOOK BELONGS TO
DIARY
UBFs 4 EVER
PUPIL

For Madeleine and Theo –RLO

For Eliza –LB

For Chloe –David O'Connell

[Imprint]
MAKE YOUR MARK

A part of Macmillan Publishing Group, LLC
120 Broadway, 25th floor, New York, NY 10271

Library of Congress Cataloging-in-Publication Data is available.

ISBN 978-1-250-77445-3 (hardcover) / ISBN 978-1-250-77447-7 (ebook)

Our books may be purchased in bulk for promotional, educational, or business use.
Please contact your local bookseller or the Macmillan Corporate and Premium Sales Department at (800) 221-7945 ext. 5442 or by email at MacmillanSpecialMarkets@macmillan.com.

Book design by Lizzie Gardiner

Illustrations by David O'Connell

Imprint logo designed by Amanda Spielman

Originally published in Great Britain by Egmont UK Limited in 2020

First American edition, 2021

1 3 5 7 9 10 8 6 4 2

mackids.com

Anyone who steals this book
Is cursed to read a map and look and look
And never find their way!
Yes this is your field trip curse.
May you always get lost . . . AND WORSE!

PIP BIRD
ILLUSTRATED BY DAVID O'CONNELL

[Imprint]
MAKE YOUR MARK
New York

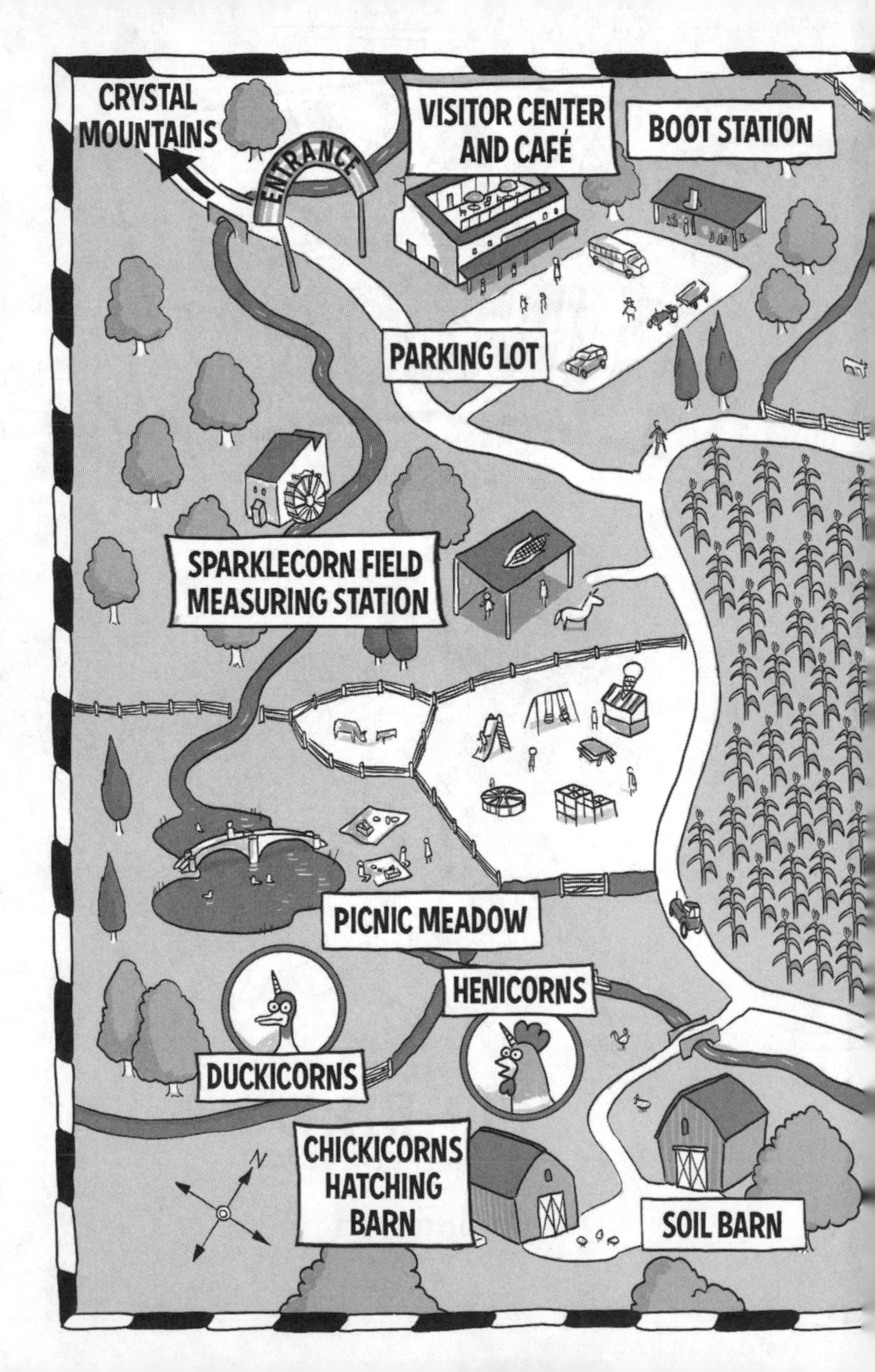
CRYSTAL MOUNTAINS
ENTRANCE
VISITOR CENTER AND CAFÉ
BOOT STATION
PARKING LOT
SPARKLECORN FIELD MEASURING STATION
PICNIC MEADOW
HENICORNS
DUCKICORNS
CHICKICORNS HATCHING BARN
SOIL BARN
N

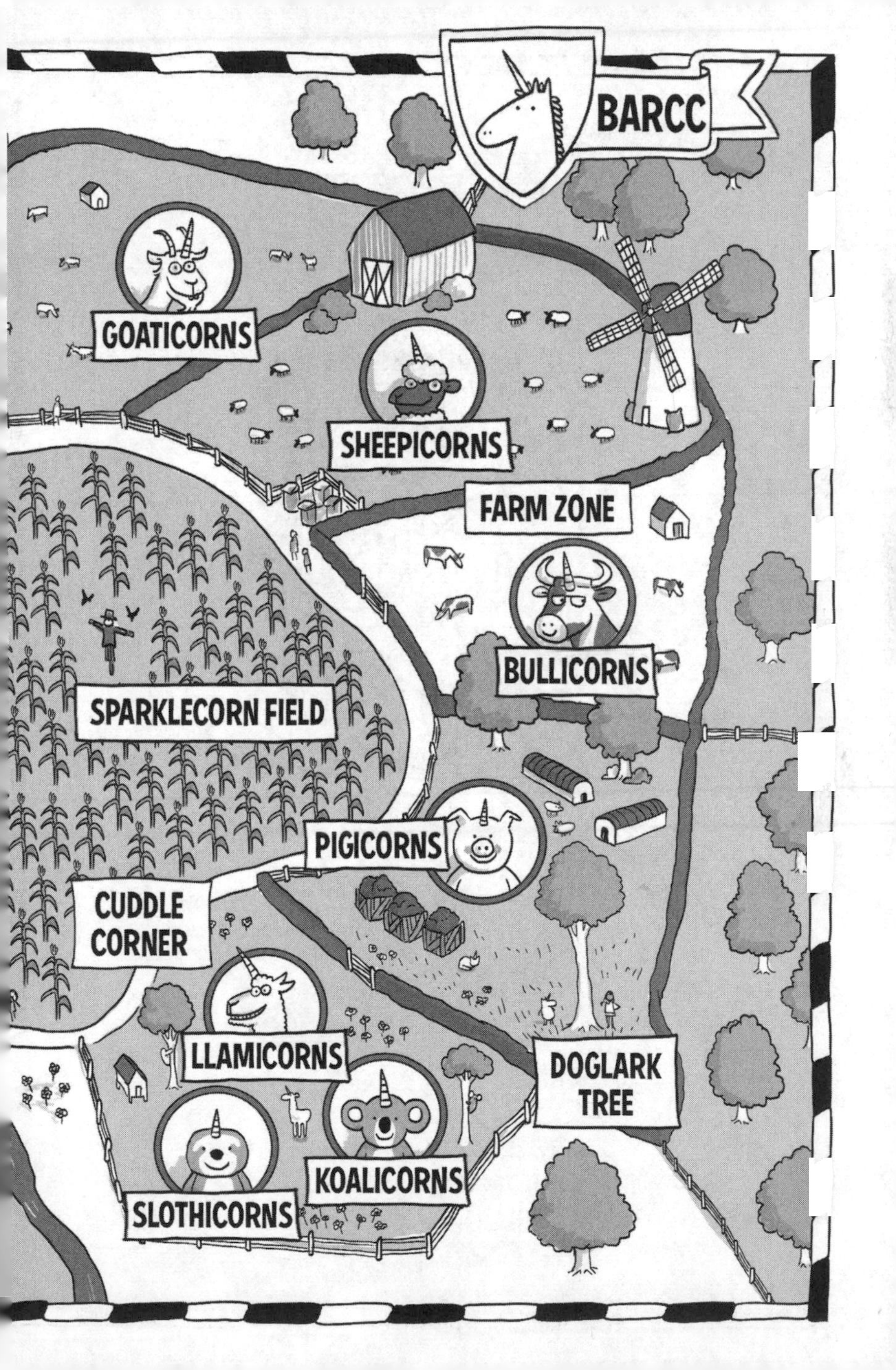
BARCC
GOATICORNS
SHEEPICORNS
FARM ZONE
BULLICORNS
SPARKLECORN FIELD
PIGICORNS
CUDDLE CORNER
LLAMICORNS
DOGLARK TREE
KOALICORNS
SLOTHICORNS

Contents

SWOONICORN

CHAPTER ONE
Tick Tock, Tick Tock

Tick tock, tick tock, BRRRRRRRRRRRRRR!

"Good morning, Rani!" said Mira, as her big sister opened her eyes.

"GGAAAARRRRRGH!" Rani screamed. "Why are you in my face?!"

Mira threw down the alarm clock and started jumping up and down on her sister's bed. "We've got to get to Unicorn School! It's MY FIELD TRIP TODAY!" Mira yelled. She was waving her signed permission slip in the air. "I'm almost ready! I just need to make my packed lunch."

"Get OFF!" Rani shoved Mira off the bed and stuck her head under the pillow.

Mira jumped onto the floor, hopping from foot to foot. "What do you think I should have in my sandwiches, tuna or cheese?"

"GO AWAY!" Rani flung a pillow at her little sister.

"Okay, bye! See you downstairs!" Mira dodged the pillow and scooped up their cat, Pickles, for a cuddle on the way.

Soon, she'd be cuddling Dave, her UBFF (Unicorn Best Friend Forever). He was the best unicorn in the world. Sure, he could be pretty grumpy. And he ALWAYS wanted to eat snacks or take a nap, and this often got them both

in trouble. And he certainly wasn't as glittery as some of the other unicorns. (He was much more farty.) BUT Dave was Mira's UBFF and they always ended up having the most amazing adventures and TONS of fun.

Unicorn School was Mira's favorite place in the whole world. They went on quests around the Fearsome Forest, hung out with Darcy and Raheem and their unicorns, AND earned medals. She couldn't wait to go back!

UUU

After Mira had made her sandwiches (she'd decided on cheese) and had some breakfast, it was time to get dressed.

"I wish I could wear my kitticorn pajamas to

school, Pickles," Mira said, stroking the picture of the adorable kitticorn on her PJs. A kitticorn was a supercute baby cat that had a horn just like a unicorn. She'd found a book about them in the Unicorn School library and ever since then she'd been OBSESSED—drawing tons of pictures of them, keeping a list of her Top Ten Kitticorn Facts, and making her very own kitticorn toy out of cotton wool and a toilet paper roll (even though Rani said it looked more like a weird pig).

Mira was longing to meet

a kitticorn in real life, but they were VERY rare. She was planning to ask the Unicorn School teachers if they'd ever seen one. But first she had to get to Unicorn School!

As soon as Mira and Rani were dressed, it was time to leave. Rani was still grumbling about having to get up so early, but Mira was so excited about her very first Unicorn School trip that she chatted nonstop in the car on the way to the Magic Portal, and all the way around the supermarket.

Most people brought their unicorns treats like hay or carrots. But Dave liked doughnuts best of all. Unfortunately, the store didn't have any doughnuts, so Mira bought some vanilla cream

cookies instead. She'd read that vanilla creams were a kitticorn's favorite food, and so she was sure Dave would like them, too! They were on sale, so she got five packages.

Mira checked and double-checked her bag for her packed lunch and permission slip. She didn't want anything to get in the way of her first field trip. She didn't even know where they were going yet! It was all so exciting.

When they arrived at the Magic Portal, it wasn't as busy as usual. It was only Mira's class, Class Red, that had a field trip and had to arrive super early. There was something extra special about being at the portal before most other people had gotten there, and before the sun

was even fully up. It felt like going on vacation!

"Have a wonderful school trip, Mira!" said Mom, giving her a big hug, while Rani yawned loudly in her ear.

"Thanks, Mom. Oh look, there's Raheem!" Mira ran toward Raheem while waving back at her mom. "See you sooooooon!"

Raheem was one of Mira's best friends at Unicorn School. Along with Darcy, the three of them always had incredible adventures. Raheem was clutching his briefcase and looking a little bleary-eyed. Mira sprinted over and knocked him off-balance with a huge hug.

"Woohoo! Are you ready for this?!" she yelled in his ear.

"Um, yes, hello!" Raheem mumbled through a yawn.

"Then LET'S GO!" Mira dragged Raheem over to the portal, which was in some bushes behind the trash cans. On the way she listed her top five favorite kitticorn colors, to wake him up a little. When they reached the

bushes, Mira reached out for the sparkles and—

ffffzzzzz **whumpfffff**

Twinkly lights exploded around them as they zoomed upward, as if they were being sucked up a spiral slide by a rainbow vacuum cleaner. As quickly as they whooshed upward, they were suddenly hurtling back down again. Soft pink and gold rays of the rising sun shone in their eyes as they tumbled onto the landing haystack and rolled out into the Grand Paddock.

Mira took a deep breath and looked around. Right away she spotted something new. Next to the landing haystack was a big rainbow-colored BUS!

"Do you think that's for the field trip? I can't wait to find out where we're going!" Mira squealed, squeezing Raheem in excitement.

Just then, they heard a—

"TA-DAAA!" It was Darcy, spinning over to them with a wheelie. She gave Mira and Raheem high fives. "Hi, team. Missed you! Shall we find our—"

Before Darcy had a chance to finish, two unicorns came cantering over. Star and Brave were Darcy's and Raheem's unicorns, and today they were wearing the presents that Darcy and Raheem had made them on an earlier visit to Unicorn School. Brave was wearing Raheem's special homemade superhero cape, while Star was in a wig that Darcy had made her so they would have matching hair.

Star and Brave gave their humans a nuzzle. But where was Dave?

Mira looked around for her Unicorn Best Friend Forever. Down the hill, the school turrets and clock tower gleamed in the rising sun. Beyond the school, Mira could see the Fearsome Forest, and beyond that the sparkly Crystal Mountains. It was all so magical, but there was still no sign of Dave.

Miss Glitterhorn, the Class Red teacher, appeared by the side of the bus, yawning and drinking from a very big mug of tea. She put the tea down and clapped her hands.

"Good morning, Class Red!" she called.

"Gooooood mooooorrrning, Miss Glitterhorrrrn," called the children, sounding more tired than usual.

"Hi, Mom!" shouted Flo, who'd fallen asleep and woken up with a start.

"Please line up with your unicorns for the field trip," said Miss Glitterhorn. "We are leaving shortly. Have your permission slips ready!"

Mira quickly checked—yes, she still had her permission slip. But where was her unicorn? She didn't want him to miss the field trip!

"Dave? Da-ave!" Mira called quietly, ducking behind the bus to see if she could spot him.

Colin the Caretaker was filling up the bus with

rainbow-berry juice. The pump was attached to a long line of tubes all coming from different rainbow-berry trees at the edge of the forest.

Colin suddenly looked confused. He took the pump out of the bus and shook it. It looked like the juice had dried up.

There was a sudden *slurp* sound behind her. Mira looked around and saw a plump unicorn butt poking out of the rainbow-berry trees. *There* was her unicorn!

"Dave!" she whispered.

The little unicorn turned and gave her

a wave with his front hoof. He had one of the pipes in his mouth and was guzzling up the rainbow-berry juice!

"There you are!" Mira said with a giggle and ran over to give him a big hug.

By distracting Dave with a slightly sticky candy she found in her pocket, Mira managed to get the pipe off him and reconnect it to the pump. Colin started whistling happily as the juice began flowing into the bus again. Dave gave a series of cheerful burps.

"Dave, we have to line up with the others. We're going on a trip today!" Mira tried to wipe off the rainbow-berry stains from around Dave's mouth with the end of her sleeve, but she just

ended up covered in the berry juice, too. "That's a little better. Come on!"

Usually Mira had to drag Dave everywhere because he was either asleep or he would sit down and refuse to move. But right now Dave seemed very overexcited. Mira wondered if it was because of all the supersweet rainbow-berry juice and the candy. Instead of just trotting back to the bus, Dave zoomed backward and forward across the grass, knocking into trees and still burping loudly. Then he started doing all his best prancing moves. Eventually Mira managed to push the little prancing unicorn around to the bus just as Miss Glitterhorn was crossing the last of her classmates off the register.

"And, good! That's everyone. Oh!" said Miss Glitterhorn. "Dave—you look . . . rather unusual this morning?"

Mira looked closely at her unicorn. His mane had turned rainbow-colored. It must have been the rainbow-berry juice!

"Um, Dave just wanted to . . . look nice for the field trip?" Mira said. She hoped her teacher wouldn't ask any more questions.

"How lovely," said Miss Glitterhorn vaguely.

Phew, thought Mira. Surely soon they would find out where they were going and then the field trip could begin!

CHAPTER TWO

All Aboard the Rainbow Bus!

The Unicorn School principal, Madame Shetland, joined Miss Glitterhorn at the bus.

"Welcome back to Unicorn School, Class Red," yawned Madame Shetland. "Are you ready for your first field trip?"

They all cheered and Darcy started the wave.

"Yes, it is very exciting," agreed Madame Shetland sleepily. "Especially as this field trip will also involve a special quest."

A ripple of excitement ran through Class Red. Mira wondered if there would be an opportunity to win a medal!

Madame Shetland shushed the class. "So, today you will be going to BARCC. Miss Glitterhorn will tell you all you need to know on the way there."

Raheem nudged Mira. "We have to . . . bark? Like a dog? I'm a little scared of dogs."

"WOOF!" barked Flo.

Mira was almost too excited to speak. "No, no!" she said, hopping from one foot to the other. "BARCC stands for Baby Animal Rainbow Care Center. It's where they look after lots of animals and their babies. And

they sometimes have . . . they sometimes have . . ."

Mira could feel her cheeks flushing and her stomach was fluttering with excitement.

"What?" asked Darcy. "You look weird."

"KITTICORNS!" exploded Mira. "They're, like, the cutest things EVER!"

"Kitticorns are great," agreed Flo. "They're my fourth favorite animals after sloths, llamas, and goblins."

"Meh," said Darcy. "I'm a dog person. Kittens stare at you with those creepy eyes that are too big for their faces, you know? Like, what are they thinking?"

Mira frowned at her friend. "Darcy, they are the

cutest things EVER. Did you know, kitticorns can be all colors of the rainbow, but the *official* cutest ones are gold? They're very rare and superspecial."

Dave snorted loudly and shook his rainbow mane.

"Oh, you're superspecial too, Dave," said Mira quickly, giving him a comforting pat. "But kitticorns are THE most special supercute special things in the ENTIRE WORLD."

Dave looked annoyed and farted.

"If you say so, Mira," said Darcy with a shrug. "There'd better be a gift shop at this place."

Miss Glitterhorn clapped her hands. "Now, have you all got your packed lunches?"

"I DO!" Mira shouted, waving her lunch

box in the air. It was newly covered in kitticorn stickers. Inside were the cheese sandwiches she'd made earlier, plus an apple, an orange, and a box of raisins. Plus, her mom had let her have a bag of potato chips AND a chocolate cookie. And she had all the vanilla creams for Dave.

"We've *all* got lunch boxes, Mira," scoffed Jake, rolling his eyes. "My dad put FOUR chocolate cookies in mine."

Mira stuck her tongue out at Jake. He always had to brag about *something*.

The teacher clapped her hands. "Okay, time to get on the bus! On you g—Yes, Darcy?"

Darcy put her hand up. "Miss, I need to go to the bathroom," she said.

"Does anyone else need to use the bathroom?" asked Miss Glitterhorn.

Everyone except Flo put their hands up.

"Right, everyone quickly go to the stableyard to use the bathrooms there," Miss Glitterhorn instructed. "Please make sure your unicorns have had a chance to go as well."

Mira lined up with the rest of her class for the bathrooms, then took Dave over to the unicorn

bathroom to do his business. Unicorn poops were usually small and glittery, but not Dave's. He made giant sloppy poops which took Mira a long time to clean up. Mira was worried they might miss the bus, so she snuck Dave a cookie from her lunch box to hurry him up. She was pleased to see that he DID like vanilla creams.

"Dave, you and kitticorns have something in common—you BOTH love the same cookies!" she told him happily.

Dave frowned and spat the vanilla cream out on the floor. They both looked at it, and Dave ate it again. And then he made a giant poop. Mira sighed. She whipped out the foldable poop shovel she now always carried in her pocket and got to work.

Miss Glitterhorn was looking at her watch and tapping her foot when the class returned to the bus. "Good, right, children. We really must be going now. Yes, Flo?"

Flo put her hand down. "I need to go to the bathroom."

Miss Glitterhorn sighed loudly. "Why didn't you go when everyone else did?"

"I was busy braiding Sparkles's hair," Flo explained. "She wanted to look nice for the trip." Flo's unicorn, Sparkles, flicked her fishtail braid over one shoulder.

"Okay! Fine," said Miss Glitterhorn. "Quickly, please, go and use the bathroom. Everyone else, please put on a high-visibility vest. We

need to be able to spot you around the farm."

Colin the Caretaker brought out a box of neon-yellow vests. Jake got to it first and spent a while rummaging through the box.

"Jake, hurry up, please," said Miss Glitterhorn. She was starting to sound exasperated.

"I just want to make sure I get the best one," said Jake.

"They're all identical, Jake," said Darcy, wheeling over and grabbing the top one off the pile. "It's how you wear them that matters."

Everyone put one on, including the unicorns.

Finally Class Red and their unicorns all filed onto the bus.

Jake was pushing past everyone, trying to get

to the backseat. "Everyone knows that the cool people sit at the back," he said.

Mira had wanted to get the backseats for her, Raheem, and Darcy, but Jake was too quick. He scrambled on board, dragging his unicorn Pegasus with him, and jumped onto the backseat, next to Tamsin and her unicorn, Moondance.

"YES!" yelled Jake. "Me and Pegasus are the BEST at buses!"

"Get comfortable, everyone," called Miss Glitterhorn from the front. "It's a long journey."

"Once we were going on vacation and the car journey was eight hours," said Jake smugly.

"Once I got so carsick I threw up all over my mom's head," said Tamsin, next to him.

Jake stood up in alarm.

"No switching seats! Sit down please, Jake," said Miss Glitterhorn.

Mira, Raheem, and Darcy all found seats, one behind the other. Mira leaned over to buckle Dave's seat belt and accidentally tickled his tummy. Dave started to do his Dave laugh, which was a loud HAW HAW sound that Raheem found a bit frightening, but Mira thought was one of the best sounds in the world. She tickled his belly again, and Dave laughed loudly.

Once the whole class was in their seats, the doors closed. And finally they set off up Unicorn School Drive, into the Fearsome Forest!

"Woohoo, field trip!" shouted Darcy, flinging her hands in the air.

Seb and his unicorn, Firework, started beatboxing while the class chanted, "Field! Trip! Field! Trip!" Except Flo, who was yelling, "Sloths, sloths, sloths!"

Miss Glitterhorn clapped her hands several times to get their attention. "Please stop cheering, so I can make the safety announcements!" she shouted.

"Yay!" cheered Raheem.

"First, please stay seated on the bus at all

times with your seat belts on," Miss Glitterhorn said.

Darcy's hand shot up. "But, miss, you're standing," she said.

Miss Glitterhorn sighed. "I will sit as soon as I have completed the announcements, thank you, Darcy."

"Maybe you could hook your seat belt around your leg?" said Darcy helpfully.

"Thank you, Darcy. Anyway!" said Miss Glitterhorn. "We are on our way to BARCC. This is a very important field trip to learn all about the animals in our world and how to take care of them—"

Both Jake and Darcy had their hands up.

"What about the quest?" asked Jake.

"Yes, there will be a quest," said Miss Glitterhorn. "This will be explained in more detail when we're there. Mira, do you have a question?"

Mira had her hand up as far as it would go and was waving it around wildly. "Are there kitticorns at BARCC?" she blurted out.

An *ooooooh* rippled around the bus.

Miss Glitterhorn smiled. "Well, I believe that there currently *are* caticorns at BARCC, which means there might also be kitticorns! So, if we're very lucky, we just might see them. BUT they are very shy animals, so don't get your hopes up."

Mira squealed and leaned forward to talk to

Darcy. "Even Rani didn't see any kitticorns when she went to BARCC. I can't believe we might get to see some of the most awesome, cute creatures in the whole world!"

"They can't possibly be cuter than us, Star," said Darcy, and she took a quick selfie with her unicorn on her phone.

The road was getting a little bumpy and Miss Glitterhorn gripped the seats in front of her to stay on her feet.

"Oops!" she said. "Where was I? So, what's really important about this trip to BARCC is that we learn how to care for our animal friends and the world around us. So, pay attention at the center and—whooooaaaa!"

The bus turned a sharp corner and Miss Glitterhorn tumbled onto the front seat.

Everyone giggled, but Mira stared out the window, lost in a daydream where she was cuddling lots of gorgeous, furry kitticorns . . .

CHAPTER THREE

Are We Nearly There Yet?

Class Red had been on the bus for an hour already and were nearly at the top of the Crystal Mountains. Mira turned around to look through the back window of the bus. Behind them lay the Fearsome Forest. They'd never been this far away from Unicorn School before!

For the last twenty minutes they had been playing lots of fun games, including Burp Alphabet (which Miss Glitterhorn had quickly

banned). Now they were playing a game called Would You Rather?, which Mira's sister had taught her.

"Would you rather have a butt for a face or a face for a butt?" said Darcy. Most people went for a butt face.

"Would you rather have a pet sloth or a pet kitticorn?" said Mira. Everyone except Flo said that one was really hard.

"Would you rather eat poop or wear a hat made of poop forever?" said Darcy. Most people chose a poop hat.

"Would you rather have a pet kitticorn or a UBFF?" said Freya, and all the unicorns snorted crossly. Everyone said UBFF, except Mira who

said "Fluff" because she was daydreaming about what she would call her pet kitticorn.

"Would you rather eat poop or have *Dave* as your UBFF?" said Jake, with a mean grin.

Everyone gasped and looked at Mira and Dave.

"Actually, maybe Scamp . . . what?" said Mira, still in her daydream.

"I would rather eat poop than sit next to *Jake*!" said Darcy, defending Mira and Dave.

"Well I would rather LIVE in poop than sit next to you!" Jake called back.

"Well I would rather be MADE OF poop than have to sit next to YOU!" shouted Darcy.

Then Miss Glitterhorn said that all games

mentioning poop were banned and why didn't they play something nice like I Spy.

"I spy something beginning with *P*," said Darcy.

Miss Glitterhorn gave her a warning look.

Soon it was Mira's turn.

"I spy . . ." said Mira, "something beginning with . . . *S*."

"Sloths?" guessed Flo.

"No."

"Spiders?" Freya called out. Brave, Raheem's unicorn, whimpered. He was just a teensy little bit scared of spiders.

"Nope!" said Mira.

Freya tried again. "Snow-capped mountain?"

Raheem tutted. "That doesn't count as an *s*, because *mountain* begins with a—"

"Yes, that's right!" said Mira quickly. "Your turn!"

The bus started going down the other side of the Crystal Mountains. The road was steep and very twisty.

Freya thought for a minute. "I spy . . . something beginning with . . ."

"Ssssss," said Tamsin.

"It's MY turn!" said Freya with a frown.

"Can't we have another letter?" said Raheem.

"Ssssick!" Tamsin

was groaning and looked rather green. She was clutching her tummy. "I feel sick. Miss! I feel sick."

Miss Glitterhorn quickly ushered Tamsin to the front and gave her a bag to be sick in. "Will someone please swap seats with Tamsin?" she asked.

Dave was already moving back to sit in Tamsin's seat. Mira quickly followed him.

Jake grumbled as he moved to let them sit down. "Make sure your unicorn doesn't fart near Pegasus," he said. "It upsets him."

Mira gave Dave a protective pat, and Dave let out a gigantic fart. Pegasus turned to face the window. Then Flo popped her head over the seat in front, quickly followed by her unicorn, Sparkles. Flo started asking Mira a million questions about the kitticorns.

“What do they eat? Where do they sleep? Which eats more, a kitticorn or a puppicorn? What do they like to play with?”

Mira took a deep breath and answered. “Kitticorn treats, somewhere warm and smelly, a puppicorn, and balls of rainbow wool. Kitticorns can bounce the balls on their noses!”

Flo squeaked. "Sooo adorable!"

"Yup," agreed Mira with an enormous grin. "I have a book called *Kitti-cornucopia*. I can't believe we are going to get to snuggle and cuddle them and kiss their little kitticorny faces!"

Something suddenly hit the side of Mira's head. It was her apple. She turned to see Dave had opened her lunch box. Dave picked up the apple again and threw it in the air, trying to bounce it on his nose. This time it flew across the backseats and landed on Pegasus's horn. Mira leaned over, pulled the apple free, and put it back in her lunch box.

"Psst," Raheem whispered, to get Mira's attention. "What do you think the quest is?

Miss Glitterhorn didn't really say anything. Do you think it's a test?"

"I don't know. I'm sure it will be fine, Raheem," said Mira.

Darcy waved her hand in the air. "Miss, are we nearly there yet?"

Miss Glitterhorn sighed. "No, Darcy. We're about halfway. Look, here's the map of BARCC to study in the meantime."

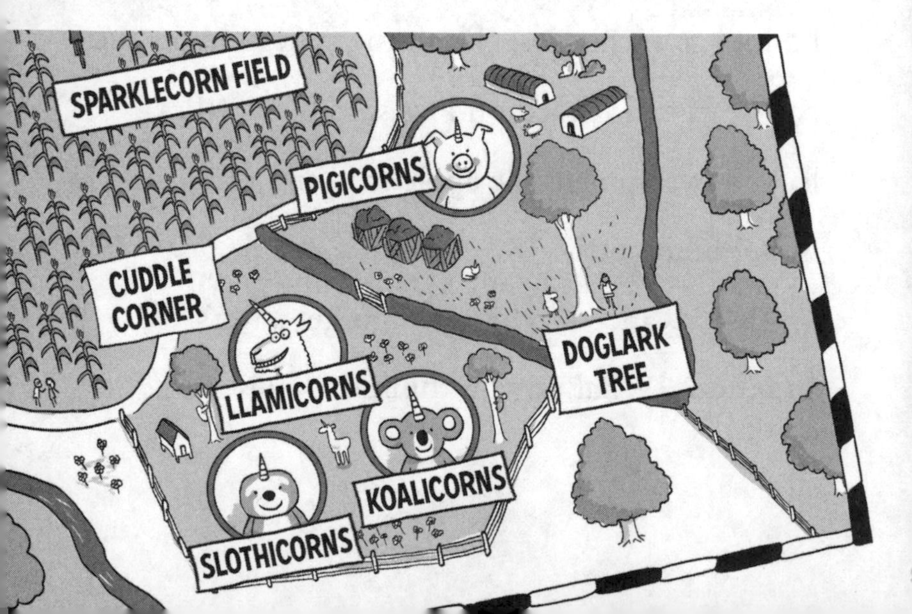

Mira spotted BARCC first. Sunlight was glinting off the gold-rimmed rainbow sign on the gates.

"We're here! We're here!" she cried.

The rest of Class Red stood up to see, and Miss Glitterhorn had to ask them to sit down again. Colin the Caretaker tooted the Rainbow Bus horn as they passed through the farm gates, and everybody cheered. As soon as the bus stopped, all the students and unicorns scrambled off the bus.

"Come back, class!" Miss Glitterhorn was trying to get everyone to line up back at the bus. "Mira, stop jumping up and down."

"WHERE ARE THE KITTICORNS?!" Mira yelled.

"And also calm down, please," said the teacher.

"Well, hello there, kids, you must be Class Red from Unicorn School!" said a voice.

"What is THAT?" Darcy looked appalled as she wheeled off the ramp.

A muddy green tractor, pulling a large trailer, tooted its horn and pulled to a stop next to the Rainbow Bus. Out jumped a short, wide man with large socks rolled over his hiking boots, long straggly hair, and a wiry gray beard. He had his hands on his hips and lots of things sticking out of pockets all over his shirt and shorts.

"Good morning, everyone! I'm Bruce Hasselhoof, chief warden here at the Baby Animal Rainbow Care Center. Let's get ready to rumble!"

Raheem shivered and nudged Mira. "I don't want to rumble."

Mira tried to give him a reassuring pat on the shoulder, but she couldn't stop grinning at the thought of kitticorns being somewhere nearby!

"We have a superexciting day planned for you all. We're going to take a tour around the farm in this tractor trailer, stop and get off for the morning's awesome activity, then have lunch, and then enjoy this afternoon's awesome activity," Bruce explained.

Darcy's hand shot up. "What are the awesome activities?"

"It's a surprise!" said Bruce, winking at Darcy.

"Is it really true that there are kitticorns here?"

Mira asked. She had stopped jumping but was now hopping from foot to foot.

Bruce smiled. "Yes! There is a caticorn here with her kitticorns. But they're tucked away somewhere, safe in their nest. Caticorns are easily scared, you know!" He clapped his hands. "Come on into the yard, kids, and get some boots on you and your unicorns. There's a lot of mud around!"

Bruce and Miss Glitterhorn started ushering the children past the tractor and over to the boot station.

Dave sniffed loudly and started trotting in the opposite direction, toward the Visitor Center and café. Mira gave him some potato chips to tempt him back to the boots. After wrestling with his

hooves for a long time, she decided that three out of four boots wasn't too bad and gave up on the last one.

Everyone else had already gathered by the

tractor trailer, where Bruce was splitting Class Red into groups of four and handing out clipboards. Raheem hugged his clipboard to his chest like it was a comfort blanket.

Bruce ushered the children and unicorns into the tractor trailer. Mira was in a group with Darcy, Raheem, and Jake. Darcy and Jake made faces at each other.

"Right!" called Bruce with a great big smile. "So, you can use your clipboard to jot down stuff you see and draw pictures—whatever you like. Awesome activity number one, here we come!"

"What about the health and safety briefing?" asked Raheem.

"Oh! Yes," said Bruce. "Well, the first rule at BARCC is to stay where I can see you at all times."

Raheem happily wrote the rule down on his clipboard.

Bruce carried on. "And the second rule at BARCC is do NOT take the baby animals home. No matter how cute they are, BARCC is the best place for them!"

"What about the quest?" asked Jake. "Can I be leader?"

Bruce laughed. "You're a keen bean, I like you," he said. Mira rolled her eyes at Darcy. "Well, there is a quest, but we don't need a leader. And anyway, no one has completed it since I did, back when I was at Unicorn School!"

Darcy gasped. "What, not in a million years?"

Bruce frowned. "I'm not quite that old, young lady." He dug out a stack of cards from one of his many pockets and started handing them out. "You can attach this to your clipboards. Don't worry if you don't have time to complete it. You'll probably be having too much fun learning all about the baby animals here at BARCC!"

BARCC QUEST. CAN YOU SPOT . . .

What is brown and sometimes sticky but is not a stick?

. . . .

What has ears but cannot hear?

. . . .

What has a bark but no bite?

. . . .

What hisses but is not a snake?

. . . .

What is an amazing sight inside which you cannot see?

. . . .

"Ooh! I love riddles," said Mira.

"This makes literally no sense," said Darcy.

"I thought nothing was going to bark at me," muttered Raheem.

"And, finally, the third rule at BARCC is no eating anything anywhere except the picnic meadow," said Bruce. "The baby animals here are on very specific diets, and we don't want to make them sick."

There was a loud neigh from Dave that sounded a bit like "NOOOOOOOOOOOO!"

"Good luck, children," said Miss Glitterhorn. "Now, since you'll be doing self-directed work on this trip, I'll just stay behind in the café and look after the shoes. Have fun!"

CHAPTER FOUR
Tap Tap Tap—Crack!

Mira was trying to get comfortable in the tractor trailer when she felt something tugging at her backpack. She looked around and saw Dave was nibbling on her bag strap. She quietly snuck him a cookie, hoping Bruce wouldn't notice. Even though the third rule at BARCC was no eating except in the picnic meadow, she thought one tiny vanilla cream couldn't hurt. And Dave NEVER left behind any crumbs.

The tractor started up with a loud rev and Bruce rubbed his hands together. "Right-o, kids!

This is the exciting bit. You can see on your right there is the sparklecorn field, which is at the center of the farm. As you know, this crop is turned into hay for unicorns and other animals, but it has many other amazing uses. As well as unicorn feed, it is used for unicorn bedding, arts and crafts materials, and even unicorn toilets!"

Raheem was taking notes on everything Bruce said. Nobody else was, although Flo had drawn a picture of a sloth climbing up the sparklecorn.

"Goats! Look! Left!" shouted Flo.

Everyone scooted over to the left-hand side of the trailer, making it lean dangerously on two wheels. They waved to the goats and baby goats in small fields.

Darcy giggled. "That goat is eating a boot." She pointed to a BARCC warden who was hopping on one foot, chasing a baby goat around a field. The baby did indeed have a boot in its mouth.

"It's a goaticorn," said Raheem, making a note of it on his clipboard. "And, yes, a goaticorn will eat anything if it's hungry enough."

"Just like you, Dave!" said Darcy.

Mira was about to defend her unicorn when she was distracted by Dave trying to get another cookie by opening the zipper of her backpack with his teeth.

"Now we are passing the sheepicorn station," Bruce continued. "You can see the wardens feeding the baby lambicorns with extra milk from a bottle."

"Toooooo cuuuuuute!" Flo gasped.

Bruce pointed out the cowicorns and pigicorns in the farm zone. They also passed a sign for the Cuddle Corner.

"What's that?" asked Flo.

"Oh, that's just the llamicorns, slothicorns, and

koalicorns," said Bruce. "Not as awesome as our first awesome activity."

There was only one thing cuter than koalicorns, Mira thought. MAYBE they were going to find and play with the kitticorns as their first activity! That really *would* be awesome.

"Here we are!" announced Bruce.

The tractor pulled up at two red barns and the children excitedly helped their unicorns out of the trailer. There were flecks of rainbow straw

lying around the door of one barn. Raheem immediately started sketching the barn on the piece of paper on his clipboard.

Bruce strode to the front of the group, unlatched the door, and pulled back the barn door to reveal . . .

"It's just full of dirt," said Mira. "Where are the animals?"

Bruce laughed. "There are LOTS of tiny animals in here, but they're just too small to see.

This is the Soil Barn! Awesome activity number one is . . . soil sieving! We're going to look very carefully at what the soil is made of and how it supports life on the farm."

"Are you joking?" asked Darcy.

Cheep cheep!

"What was that?" asked Mira.

"Oh, that's just the chickicorn hatching barn next door," said Bruce. "Now, my favorite thing about soil—"

Bruce didn't have time to finish, as Class Red stampeded over to the chickicorn barn. He only just made it to the doors before them.

"STOP! Stay with the soil!" he screeched.

Rainbow-colored straw fluttered out into

the farmyard with a chorus of *cheep-cheeping*. Class Red surged forward again.

"Well, I suppose we can have a quick look before we start soil sieving," said Bruce with a sigh. "So *this* is the chickicorn hatching barn."

There were bales of rainbow straw piled up on each side of the barn, and different-colored henicorns sitting on eggs in nests. At the far end there were two long tables with rows of lights dangling above them. Under each light was a carefully made rainbow nest with one or two eggs inside.

"Chickicorns hatch when their eggs are warm and cozy. Now, some of our henicorns lay so many eggs they can't sit on them all. That's

why we have these hot lights over some nests. It's called incubating," explained Bruce. "And it's very important that no one disturbs the incubating process. Otherwise the chickicorns could hatch and become confused. So don't touch anything!"

Class Red gathered around the hatching tables.

"Is anything actually going to happen?" asked Darcy.

"Shh," said Bruce. "Yes, if we're quiet, we just might hear an egg cracking."

The children waited.

The eggs stayed very still.

"I don't hear anything," said Darcy again.

"SHH!" said Bruce again. "The conditions for hatching need to be just right."

As all the Class Red students stood quietly, Mira heard Dave's stomach rumble. Then, before she could stop him, he quickly licked one of the multicolored eggs!

"Dave, no!" Mira hissed. "It's an egg, not a candy!"

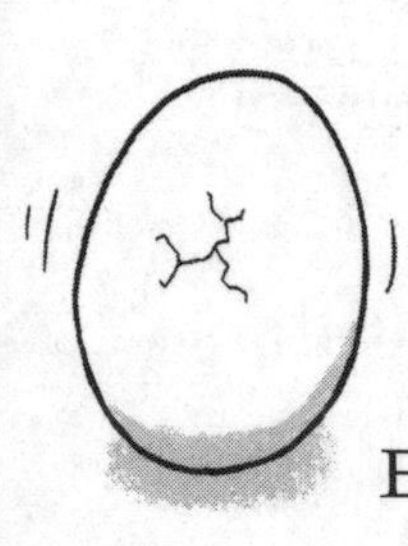

Tap tap tap.

"What's THAT?" asked Darcy.

"That's a hatching sound. SHHHH, EVERYONE!"

Mira thought Bruce's shushing was louder than Darcy's talking, but then there was another . . .

Tap tap tap—crack!

A small hole appeared in the top of the egg in front of Dave.

Tap tap crack crack tap crack TAP CRACK.

A tiny, bent horn emerged from the eggshell, followed by a pale-blue fluffy chickicorn. It gave an adorable *cheep* and shook the rest of the shell off its back. It stared at Dave.

Dave stared at it. Then the chickicorn jumped onto Dave's nose and nestled in his mane.

Cheep! it cheeped.

"Awww," said Flo. "It thinks your hair is rainbow straw!"

Dave shook his head. The chickicorn rolled back down his nose and into the nesting box. It sat up, hopped up Dave's nose, and snuggled into his mane again. Dave kept shaking his head, but the chickicorn was clinging on tightly now with its beak.

CHEEP! it cheeped happily.

Dave seemed to have started a trend. There was more tapping and cracking, and lots of

colorful little fluffy chickicorns were hatching all over the table and jumping all over the place.

"I've never seen so many hatch at once!" cried Bruce in a panic. "Quick, we've got to get the babies back into their nests!"

Class Red didn't need telling twice. They all started running around, trying to catch the baby chickicorns and scoop them back into their nests.

By the time they'd rounded up all the chickicorns, the morning was almost over.

"No time for soil sieving," said Bruce, shaking his head sadly.

"Oh no," said Darcy.

"You're right—it's a real shame," said Bruce,

brightening up. "Maybe I can swap the afternoon activity—"

"NO!" shouted Class Red.

Everyone saw Bruce's face fall.

"We mean, you just explained it so well," said Mira quickly. "We've all noted down lots of facts and drawn the soil."

The class nodded.

"I actually have done that," said Raheem.

"That's great!" said Bruce, looking pleased. "I guess it's time for lunch, then."

At the word *lunch*, there was a loud SMASH, as Dave bolted through the barn doors and raced toward the trailer.

CHAPTER FIVE
Picnic Time

Everyone was very pleased to get to the picnic field (and to get out of the soil sieving). They were having their lunch in a wildflower meadow, where red-and-white checked picnic blankets had been laid out. Next to the field there was a little pond with a bridge over it, with a family of duckicorns swimming around. In the field to the right was a bullicorn and its baby. Even though the animals were grazing peacefully, they were still a little on the scary side with their red eyes and sharp horns.

Class Red lined up to collect a bag of hay for their unicorns. Then they all sat down on the picnic blankets and opened up their lunch boxes.

Jake was sitting behind Mira, Raheem, and Darcy with his unicorn, Pegasus.

"Hey!" shouted Jake. "Dave's eaten three of my four chocolate cookies!"

Mira turned around and looked in Jake's lunch box. There were indeed three empty chocolate cookie wrappers. She looked at Dave, who was licking his lips. There was a large smear of chocolate on his nose.

"Well," said Mira. "You can't prove it was Dave."

"I actually saw him eat them," said Jake.

“I’ll swap you a cookie for your potato chips,” said Seb.

“Great teamwork, everyone!” said Bruce, clapping his hands.

“I’ll swap you a sandwich for my cookie,” added Darcy.

Jake smiled. “Fine, here you go,” he said, handing her a square of sandwich.

Darcy shook her head. "No, the whole thing."

"But that's not fair!" protested Jake.

Darcy shrugged. "Come back to me when you have a serious offer."

Mira gave Dave a whole packet of vanilla creams to stop him from stealing any more lunches. Then she noticed that Raheem and Brave weren't eating their lunch and were staring intently at the clipboard.

"Are you okay?" asked Mira.

"We're just looking at the quest list to see if we can solve some of the riddles," said Raheem. "I'm sure we'll have spotted some things already."

"I'm not that worried about the quest," said Mira, sharing her sandwich with Dave. "Even

though I *would* like to get a medal. But mostly I just want to see a kitticorn."

Flo sighed into her bag of potato chips. "Me too."

"Did you know kitticorn horns are soft and furry when they're first born?" Mira said.

"Nooooooo!"

"Yes!" said Mira happily. "And if they're feeling playful, they tickle your face with their tail."

Mira took a sip of her juice and tried to remember her next favorite kitticorn fact.

She turned back to Flo, but for some reason, Dave's butt was in her face. He swooshed his tail around.

"Bluerghle argle flargh!" As Mira tried to stop

Dave's tail tickling her, she spilled her juice. Dave quickly licked it up, then burped grumpily.

"Is Dave okay?" asked Flo.

"Are we playing Burp Alphabet again?" said Seb.

"I think Dave's just hungry," said Mira, giving her unicorn a bit more sandwich. "Did you know that if kitticorns want your attention, they wind around your ankles over and over again?"

There was a THUD as Dave dived over the picnic blanket and collided with Mira's ankles, knocking her over.

"Dave!" Mira said. "Calm down!" She handed him a cookie. "And," Mira went on, turning back to Flo, "if they REALLY love you, kitticorns roll over and show you their tummies for tickling."

"Awww!" said Flo.

Dave dropped to the ground, rolled over onto his back, and kicked his legs in the air. Unfortunately, as his legs flailed around, he kicked Sparkles in the nose. Sparkles snorted, stepped back, tripped over Jake's lunch box, and fell into his lap, squashing his last cookie.

"Arghh, you're all SO annoying!" shouted Jake, pushing Sparkles away.

"Do you think Dave is trying to tell you something?" asked Flo thoughtfully.

"No," said Mira. "He's just being Dave."

Dave plopped himself down on the picnic blanket. For a moment Mira thought he looked sad. Was Flo right?

"MEEARRGH!" whinnied Dave suddenly, and shook his head. "MEEEEEEEARGH!"

Mira stared at him. It was the strangest sound she'd ever heard.

"Maybe he's trying to tell you that he's got a chickicorn in his mane," said Flo, nibbling on a potato chip.

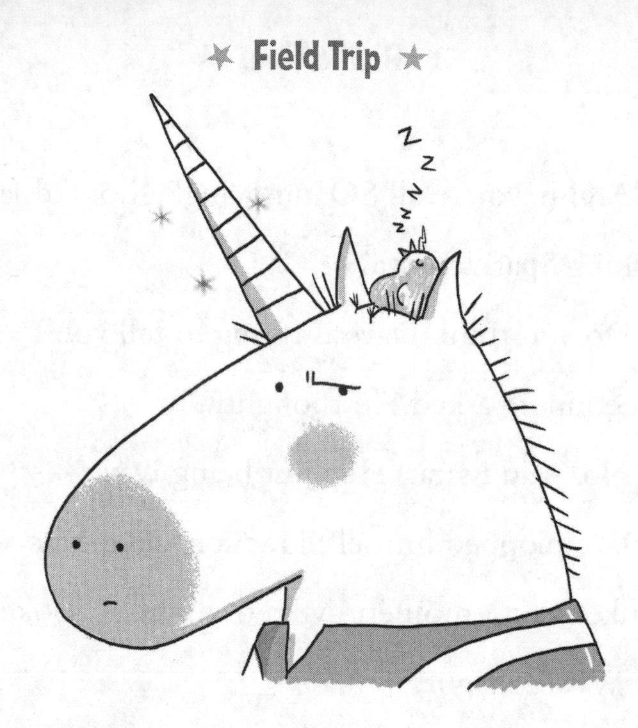

"WHAT?!"

Mira rushed over to Dave and checked.

Sure enough, there was a baby blue chickicorn snoozing in Dave's mane. It looked very cozy.

"Dave, how did this happen?" Mira said.

Dave shrugged. The chickicorn woke up and *cheep*ed.

"The second rule of BARCC is not to take any of the baby animals," said Raheem worriedly.

Mira gulped. They hadn't *meant* to take the chickicorn, but what if they got in trouble for breaking the rules? What if they didn't get a chance to see a kitticorn?

"We've got to get it back to its barn without Bruce seeing," Mira said.

"Everything all right over there?" Bruce called over as he packed up the picnic blankets.

The chickicorn *cheep-cheep*ed again and they all shushed it.

"Absolutely fine!" shouted Darcy. "We were just saying how much we love the soil in this wildflower meadow!"

Bruce beamed. "As you should. Okay, kids, let's get back to the trailer and get on to your second awesome activity for the day!"

"What can be more awesome than sieving soil?" asked Darcy.

"Just you wait and see!" said Bruce with a huge grin, starting up the tractor.

∪∪∪

A few minutes later Bruce stopped the tractor.

"Right-o, kids!" he said. "Here we are in the sparklecorn field. Your second awesome activity today is . . . measuring the sparklecorn!"

All the children and their unicorns slowly climbed down from the trailer. Bruce handed out

measuring tapes and charts. Raheem carefully attached the chart to his clipboard and sharpened his pencil.

"We need to measure the sparklecorn each spring to make sure it's healthy and happy. You will see on your measuring tapes the perfect height for each cornstalk," said Bruce.

Mira unfurled her tape and saw inch markings with numbers and pictures. At one yard there was a picture of a sparklecorn stalk, surrounded by lots of sparkles and words that read, *Perfect sparklecorn height*!

"Each team of four will have one square yard to measure," said Bruce. "I've marked out the areas with rainbow tape. Please measure all the sparklecorn stalks in your patch and write them down on the chart. You have one hour to complete this activity. After that, it'll be almost

time for you to go back to Unicorn School. So make the most of it! I'll just be over in the tractor if you need me."

Jake flung his arms in the air. "This is going to take forever!" he moaned. "What about the quest?"

The chickicorn cheeped loudly from inside Dave's mane and Dave frowned.

Raheem looked up from the clipboard. "Actually, I think we're doing pretty well on the quest. I've been figuring out the riddles."

"Really?" said Mira.

Raheem pointed to the checklist. "Number one was 'What is brown and sticky but is not a stick?' Well, that's awesome activity one: soil."

"*Don't* call it awesome," muttered Darcy.

"And then, 'What has ears but cannot hear?,'" continued Raheem. He pointed at the sparklecorn. "Ears of corn can't hear. I haven't figured out number three yet—'What has a bark but no bite?'"

"The farm monster?" said Darcy.

"That's stupid!" said Jake, but Mira saw him glancing around.

"Wait, what was number four?" said Mira.

"'What hisses but is not a snake?,'" said Raheem.

"I KNOW THAT ONE!" shrieked Mira. "Hissing is just one of the many adorable noises that a kitticorn makes! That must be the answer!" An idea suddenly came to her. "Bruce

said we don't have much time left. Why don't we return the chickicorn and find the kitticorns at the same time? AND we might find the missing answers and complete the quest!"

Jake grinned and punched the air. "Woo! If we complete the quest, we win the MEDAL!" Jake loved medals almost as much as Mira did.

"I'm in," said Darcy. "This is *actually* awesome."

Raheem pointed to the measuring tape. "But what about the activity? We have to measure ALL the corn."

"Leave that to me," said Darcy.

She took four cookies out of her lunch box and held them under Dave's nose. Just as he was about

to chomp them, Darcy threw one to each corner of their sparklecorn patch. Dave sped away, the little chickicorn on his head cheeping excitedly—and gobbled up all four cookies, flattening the entire patch of corn into a neat little square.

Raheem gasped.

"Our corn all comes in at zero inches," said Darcy, writing a big *0* on the clipboard with a flourish. "So, which way to the chicks?"

"And the kitticorns!" said Mira.

"And the quest!" said Jake.

"Show me the map," said Darcy. "Let's do this, Team Awesome!"

CHAPTER SIX

Quests, Chicks, and Kitticorns

"We know where the chickicorn barn is, so let's find the kitticorns first," said Jake. "Does anyone know where they might be?"

"I have LOTS of ideas," said Mira enthusiastically.

"Shall we start with one idea, maybe?" Raheem said, looking at his watch. "We have to find the kitticorns AND return the chickicorn AND complete the quest AND get back before the school bus leaves . . ."

Mira thought for a minute. "Well, kitticorns

really like to play with glitter daisies. There were a lot near the Cuddle Corner. Which way was that?"

Raheem looked at the map on his clipboard. "We probably shouldn't go on the tractor trail as we don't want Bruce to see us, so we might have to go straight through the sparklecorn field."

Jake took the map from Raheem and said it was definitely left. Darcy took it from Jake and said it was definitely right. Raheem reached over and carefully turned the map the right way up. Then he pointed to the unicorns, who had all shuffled to face the same way. (Except Dave, who was taking a nap. The chickicorn on his head had

fallen asleep, too, and was making cute little cheepy snores.)

"The unicorns are pointing north," said Raheem. "So according to the map, the Cuddle Corner is . . . that way!"

Mira woke up Dave, and everyone got onto their unicorns and headed through the sparklecorn, one behind the other. The leaves tickled Dave's ears as they brushed past the stalks, and he gave a series of giggly snorts as he wove in and out of the tall plants. The chickicorn kept sneezing.

After a few minutes, they reached the Cuddle Corner. They looked all the way around the fence twice. There were so many glitter daisies that the unicorns got sparkles all over their hooves, but they didn't see any kitticorns. Dave started snacking on the flowers and got a glittery tongue.

Jake folded his arms. "You said they'd be here," he said to Mira.

"I didn't!" Mira protested. "I said they *might* be here. Ooh, I know! Kitticorns love to snuggle up in soft wool. Maybe they'll be—"

"Near the baby lambicorns!" cried Darcy. "This way!"

Raheem pointed in the opposite direction. "It's actually over there."

"Yes, that's what I meant," said Darcy. "Follow me!" She and Star whirled around and started trotting back through the sparklecorn.

When they reached the baby lambicorns, there was plenty of wool but no kitticorns.

Jake looked very grumpy. "We're *never* going to find them and finish this quest," he said. "Let's just return the silly chickicorn and go

back to the stupid sparklecorn measuring activity."

Cheep, said the chickicorn happily.

Raheem tapped his watch. "That might be a good idea," he said.

"No!" cried Mira. "Let's try one more place. Umm . . . Where else could they be?"

As Mira thought hard, she was distracted by a strange snuffling sound. Turning around, she realized that Dave had climbed into a large trash can and was gulping down some old fries.

"Dave!" she shouted. Dave reversed out of the trash can. He was eating a fry and there was a banana peel on his horn. The chick was also eating a fry.

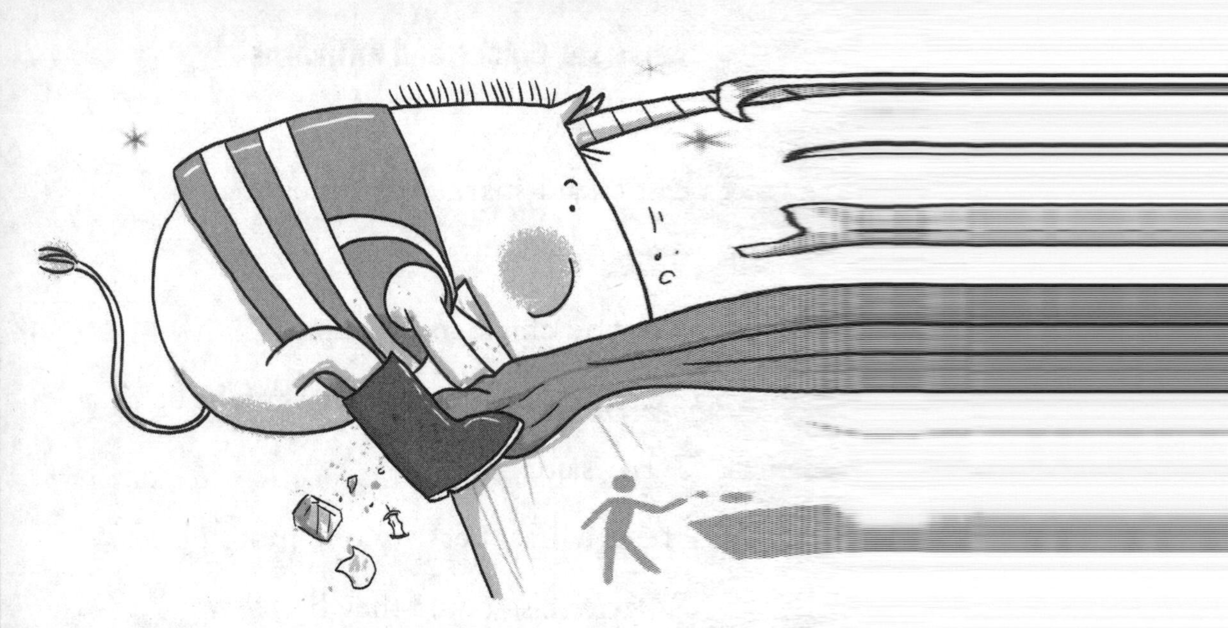

Mira suddenly had a terrific idea.

"The trash cans!" she yelled.

"What?" asked Jake.

"My book said that kitticorns like to m

nests in a nice warm place that's a bit smell

other animals from finding their nest. The

some compost bins behind the pigicorn

Mira said excitedly. "Let's give it one mo

back to the stupid sparklecorn measuring activity."

Cheep, said the chickicorn happily.

Raheem tapped his watch. "That might be a good idea," he said.

"No!" cried Mira. "Let's try one more place. Umm . . . Where else could they be?"

As Mira thought hard, she was distracted by a strange snuffling sound. Turning around, she realized that Dave had climbed into a large trash can and was gulping down some old fries.

"Dave!" she shouted. Dave reversed out of the trash can. He was eating a fry and there was a banana peel on his horn. The chick was also eating a fry.

Mira suddenly had a terrific idea.

"The trash cans!" she yelled.

"What?" asked Jake.

"My book said that kitticorns like to make their nests in a nice warm place that's a bit smelly. It stops other animals from finding their nest. There were some compost bins behind the pigicorn pens," Mira said excitedly. "Let's give it one more try,

"I didn't!" Mira protested. "I said they *might* be here. Ooh, I know! Kitticorns love to snuggle up in soft wool. Maybe they'll be—"

"Near the baby lambicorns!" cried Darcy. "This way!"

Raheem pointed in the opposite direction. "It's actually over there."

"Yes, that's what I meant," said Darcy. "Follow me!" She and Star whirled around and started trotting back through the sparklecorn.

When they reached the baby lambicorns, there was plenty of wool but no kitticorns.

Jake looked very grumpy. "We're *never* going to find them and finish this quest," he said. "Let's just return the silly chickicorn and go

Mira woke up Dave, and everyone got onto their unicorns and headed through the sparklecorn, one behind the other. The leaves tickled Dave's ears as they brushed past the stalks, and he gave a series of giggly snorts as he wove in and out of the tall plants. The chickicorn kept sneezing.

After a few minutes, they reached the Cuddle Corner. They looked all the way around the fence twice. There were so many glitter daisies that the unicorns got sparkles all over their hooves, but they didn't see any kitticorns. Dave started snacking on the flowers and got a glittery tongue.

Jake folded his arms. "You said they'd be here," he said to Mira.

and if they're not there, then we'll just return the chickicorn and go back to the bus. Pleeeeease?"

"It'll have to be a very quick look," said Raheem, looking anxious.

Mira jumped back onto Dave. "Come on, team—to the pigicorn pens!"

And they charged off through the sparklecorn as quickly as Dave's little legs could carry him, the chickicorn in his mane happily *cheep-cheep*ing away.

The pigicorn pens were easy to find, as they were in front of a very tall tree. There was a sign on the tree saying

it was a "Doglark" tree and the tallest tree on the farm. Raheem wrote this down.

"Okay everybody, let's find the compost bins NICE AND QUIETLY," said Mira, taking charge.

They trotted around the back of the pigicorn pens. The pigicorns were asleep, surrounded by old bits of food and lots of mud. Dave farted approvingly.

Prrrrrrrr.

Mira gasped. "It's a purr!" she whispered.

"Isn't it a pig fart?" whispered Darcy.

PRRRRRRRR.

The sound was coming from behind the compost bin. Mira slid off Dave and tiptoed to the bin. Dave was close behind her. She was so excited

that she took a deep breath, then regretted it because of the smell. She squeezed her eyes shut to calm down, then peeked around the bin.

There they were! A grown-up caticorn had made a nest in the long grass and was snoozing. Beside her was a litter of four rainbow-colored kitticorns and . . . Mira could hardly believe her eyes. One *GOLDEN* kitticorn!

"Awwww!" said Jake quietly.

"They actually *are* a little cute in real life," whispered Darcy.

Mira squealed in amazement. They were even more adorable than she had ever imagined. Her dream had come true!

Her squeal woke up the mother caticorn. She hissed loudly at Mira.

Mira turned to the group. "See, they do hiss!" she said happily. Then she turned back to the nest. "It's okay, beautiful kitty," she began. "I'm your best friend—"

HIISSSSSSSSSSSS! The caticorn stood up, arched her back, and narrowed her eyes at Mira.

“Um, Mira, that doesn’t sound like a happy sound . . .” said Darcy.

Mira thought that *might* be true, but she couldn’t help it. She just HAD to cuddle one! Carefully, she reached out a hand to stroke the golden kitticorn.

“Are you sure that’s a good idea?” asked Raheem, who was standing *way* back by the compost bin.

Just as Mira's fingers were about to touch the golden kitticorn's fur, the mother caticorn gave an extra loud *HISSSSSSSSSSS*, waking up the rest of the kitticorns, before she darted off behind the compost bin. The kitticorns scattered.

Mira's shoulders slumped. "Why don't the kitticorns like me?" she asked. Dave shrugged and gave Mira a nuzzle.

Mira suddenly heard Darcy giggling. She turned around to see that her friend was *covered* in kitticorns. One was perched on Darcy's shoulders, another was sitting on her boot, and one kitticorn was curled up purring on her lap.

"Stop it, you guys, that tickles!" Darcy giggled, trying to stop one of the kitticorns licking her ear.

Dave chose that moment to make a massive poop right next to Darcy, which spooked the kitticorns and made them run off.

"Phew, thanks, Dave," said Darcy, brushing pastel-colored fur off her shirt. "That was a bit much."

"Why do they like you and not me?" asked Mira. She took out her portable poop shovel and miserably cleaned up Dave's poop.

"What can I say?" asked Darcy with a flick of her hair. "I have a magnetic personality."

Even Jake was cuddling a kitticorn now. Mira had never seen him so happy! The kitticorn cuteness had gotten to him, too. Mira felt really left out.

Raheem checked his watch. "We should return the chickicorn and get back to the bus. Let's get these kitticorns back to the nest."

Mira hung back while the others rounded up the kittens and put them safely back into the caticorn's nest. The mother soon settled down happily next to them.

"Let's head back to the chickicorn barn!" said Jake, still grinning from his kitticorn cuddle.

Mira took one last, sad look at the nest. The four little rainbow kitticorns were settling down sleepily. But the mother caticorn was looking around in a worried way . . .

"Wait!" said Mira.

"You've already tried to make them like you," said Darcy impatiently. "You've just got to let it go."

"No," said Mira. "The golden kitticorn isn't in the nest!"

The mother caticorn was pacing around now and meowing loudly, calling for her missing baby. Mira swallowed guiltily. She'd been so focused on trying to cuddle the kitticorns that she'd forgotten Bruce said that caticorns were easily scared. She hadn't been very careful at all!

They looked everywhere around the bins and the pigicorn pens for any tiny little space the kitticorn could have run into. The mother caticorn's meows were getting louder and more worried. They strained their ears, but they couldn't hear the kitticorn anywhere.

What they did hear was a loud scratching sound. Dave was by the Doglark tree, scratching his butt on the trunk.

"Oh, Dave, you could at least help!" said Mira crossly.

Dave stopped. And then he ran backward at Mira and swooshed his tail in her face.

"PAH!" said Mira, trying to push Dave's tail away. "Stop it!"

Then Dave ducked his head and started running in and out of Mira's ankles. The two of them got tangled up and fell to the ground.

"What are you doing, Dave?" said Mira helplessly. "We've got to find the kitticorn—we don't have time for messing around!"

Dave sighed, then dropped to the ground on his back. He waved his hooves in the air, and then pointed straight upward.

Mira looked up.

There, on the tallest branch of the tallest tree on the farm, was the golden kitticorn.

CHAPTER SEVEN
Rescue Mission!

"Great," said Darcy. "So now we've stolen a chickicorn AND gotten a kitticorn stuck up a tree."

"AND we could miss the bus home!" said Jake crossly.

Mira felt a tear roll down her cheek. She'd been so excited to come to BARCC and meet all the animals and learn about the farm and make best friends with a kitticorn. And win an awesome quest medal. But it had all gone wrong. She sniffed and wiped her nose.

Raheem, Darcy, and Jake were all calling up

to the kitticorn. Jake was even making mewing sounds. But the golden kitticorn was very high up in the tree, and didn't seem like it was going to move anytime soon.

Mira looked for Dave. She wanted to say sorry for not realizing that he'd been trying to tell her where the kitticorn was. But she couldn't see Dave anywhere!

She realized then that she hadn't really been paying Dave much attention on this trip at all. All she had thought about were kitticorns. Dave must know she didn't love kitticorns more than him, she thought. He was her UBFF! But then she remembered Dave's sad expression at the picnic. Maybe he DID think she loved kitticorns more—and maybe that was why he'd left!

Mira started looking frantically around. The others were helping the kitticorn. *She* needed to find Dave.

"Here kitty, kitty, kitty!" called Darcy. "Come on down! We promise Mira won't try to pet you again!"

"Dave!" Mira called. "Dave, where are you? I'm sorry, Dave, come back!"

Just as Mira started to panic, she heard the sound of hooves thudding through the sparklecorn behind her. She turned around and saw Dave running as fast as his little legs could carry him. He had Mira's lunch box in his mouth.

"You came back!" Mira gave her unicorn a huge hug. Dave was out of breath from running so fast.

"I didn't notice he was gone," asked Jake. "More important, how are we going to get this kitticorn down from this massive tree?"

Dave dropped the lunch box on the ground. A packet of vanilla creams fell out.

"I thought you ate them all—oh! Dave! You're actually a genius!" Mira gasped. She gave him another hug and the little unicorn blushed.

"I don't get what's happening," said Jake. "Why is Dave a genius?"

Mira grinned widely. "Kitticorns love vanilla creams! Quick, let's see if we can persuade this little one to come down."

Mira took a vanilla cream out of the package and held it out for the golden kitticorn to see. Sure enough, the kitticorn crept to the edge of a branch and then climbed down a couple of branches.

"Yay! Keep going!" Darcy started clapping.

The kitticorn kept jumping down. Then it suddenly slipped. Mira's heart was in her mouth as it dangled from a high branch, mewing pitifully.

"We have to help it!" Jake cried. He jumped up but couldn't reach the branch. He stood on Pegasus's back and tried to reach again.

"It's still too high for you," said Darcy.

"Yes, thanks, that's really helpful," Jake muttered with a frown. "Come on, Mira. I need your help. Climb up on my shoulders."

Mira hung back. "But it doesn't like me! Can't someone else do it?"

"I'm too scared," said Raheem.

"And I'm taking a picture. Smile!" Darcy held up her phone for a group pic.

Mira took a deep breath. She knew she had to help the kitticorn. After all, if she hadn't disturbed the nest, the kitticorn

wouldn't be stuck up in the tree in the first place!

Dave nuzzled her arm and gave an encouraging fart. It was just what Mira needed.

"Thanks Dave," she said gratefully.

With the package of vanilla creams between her teeth, Mira started to clamber up onto Pegasus's back. Dave gave her a helpful shove with his muzzle. Carefully, she climbed onto Jake's shoulders. Wobbling slightly, she stretched out her arm. She *still* couldn't reach the kitticorn.

"I think we need Dave!" she called down.

"Does it have to be Dave?" said Jake, but Mira's plump little UBFF was already climbing onto

Pegasus, letting out little farts with the effort. Pegasus looked pained.

Dave eventually climbed onto Mira's shoulders. She passed him the vanilla creams and he reached up his hoof. The kitticorn hung upside down, looking at Dave and blinking. Mira could see that it was so scared it didn't know what to do.

"Come on!" Mira pleaded.

Dave farted one more time.

Startled, the kitticorn let go of the branch, fell onto Dave's nose, and wrapped its tiny paws around Dave's horn. The chickicorn popped its head out of Dave's mane and cheeped. The kitticorn squeaked and jumped, sliding off Dave and down into Mira's arms.

The kitticorn was so surprised that it lay completely still in Mira's arms for a moment. Its fur was supersoft and its little heart was beating quickly. It smelled of warm grass and vanilla creams. Despite being balanced on Jake's shoulders and a long way from the ground, Mira felt a moment of total bliss.

Then the kitticorn ran down her legs and off Jake's back. With one big leap from Pegasus's butt, it scampered away behind the pigicorn pens and back into its nest.

Dave and Mira climbed down more carefully.

Darcy and Raheem gave them all a round of applause. Mira high-fived her friends and pulled Dave close for a huge hug.

"You're the best, Dave," she whispered in her unicorn's fluffy ear. "Come on, Team Awesome, let's get that chickicorn back and go home."

MEEOW!

Mira turned to see the entire caticorn family standing in a line, staring at her. Before she could say "uh-oh," the adorable kitticorns ran in and out of her ankles, purring. Then they all dropped to the ground and flailed their legs in the air, allowing her to tickle their tummies, before disappearing back behind the bins.

"Are you about to cry again?" asked Darcy.

There was a big lump in Mira's throat as she smiled. "My book says when they do that, it means they REALLY like you!" she said.

"Honestly?" said Darcy. "More than when they give you tons of cuddles and kisses like they did for me and Jake?"

Raheem coughed. "Let's just get to the chickicorn barn, shall we?"

∪∪∪

Mira thought Dave would be a little tired after all the excitement, so she gave him some more vanilla creams for energy (after leaving some by the compost bin for the caticorn family to enjoy later).

When they reached the chickicorn hatching

barn, Mira slid the barn door open. All the chickicorns were sitting happily in their nests and cheeping. Mira picked up the chickicorn from Dave's mane and dropped it carefully into one of the rainbow-straw hatching nests.

"There you go!" she said brightly. "Just like Dave's mane. But better!"

The chickicorn looked up at her. Quick as a flash, it jumped out of the straw and hopped back up onto Dave's head.

CHEEP!

Mira tried again and again and again, but each time the chickicorn jumped back onto Dave and burrowed into his mane.

Then Mira got Dave to stand outside the barn. She picked up the chick, ran into the barn, put it down, raced back out as fast as she could, slid the barn door shut, and returned to Dave. He hung his head and snuffled.

Mira gave his ears a tickle. "Aww, I know you

liked that chick, Dave. But don't worry, it will always be right here." Mira pointed to his heart.

"No it won't," said Darcy.

"Sshh!" said Mira. "I'm trying to make Dave feel better!"

"Yes, but the chickicorn is back."

Darcy pointed. Sure enough, there was the little fluffy blue chick, perched on top of Dave's big round bottom.

"Argh! We've got to get back!" cried Mira. "What are we going to do? THIS is your home, little chickicorn!"

Darcy was inspecting her nails. "The trouble is that the chickicorn thinks Dave *is* home," she explained. "The chick jumped on him as

soon as it hatched. It thinks that Dave is its mom."

"That's it!" cried Mira. "Darcy, you're a genius!"

"Well, duh," said Darcy, fluffing her hair. "Why this time in particular?"

Mira raced back into the barn. "There you are!" she said, scooping up a sad-looking, light-blue henicorn with a bent horn. "There's someone you need to meet."

Cluck cluck cluck.

The chickicorn popped its head up from Dave's tail. *Cheep?*

Cluck!

Cheep! CHEEP!

The henicorn hopped out of Mira's arms just as the chickicorn slid down Dave's tail.

They ran toward each other in a[illegible]ry of *clucks* and *cheeps*.

The chickicorn had found its mom!

ER EIGHT

-tastic

Mira really wa of Dave. She knew it was always had saygdbye to your friends. She hated saying goto Dave when she left Unicorn School, at least she knew she was always comingbsoon. She gave her UBFF an extra big pa ey all raced back through the sparklecorn f.

Riding besidera, Raheem looked glum.

"Are you okayMira asked.

Raheem shrugd. "I just would have liked to finish the quest.

"We still had three more answers to find. It was really hard," Mira consoled her friend.

"Actually we found two more," said Raheem. "'What hisses but is not a snake?' was kitticorns, and 'What has a bark but no bite?' was the Doglark tree."

"Whoa!" said Darcy. "We finished the quest and you didn't say anything?"

"Raheem, that's awesome!" said Jake.

Raheem shook his head. "No," he said. "We still have the last riddle to solve."

Jake stopped suddenly. "Where is everyone?"

"We've missed the bus!" Raheem started to panic.

"Chill, they're in the—ARGH!" Darcy pulled Star up so quickly that the others bumped into her.

Mira started panicking now. "What's wrong? Have they left without us?"

"No," said Darcy. "Nobody told me there was a gift shop! There's no time to waste!"

They all galloped toward the shop in the visitor center, where they could see the rest of Class Red choosing pencils and erasers and cuddly horned toys. Mira breathed a sigh of relief as they joined their classmates. They'd returned the chickicorn, met lots of kitticorns, *and* hadn't missed the bus home. Phew!

Miss Glitterhorn was upstairs in the café, surrounded by empty teacups and reading a book. She looked happier than she had in weeks.

Seb and his unicorn, Firework, were trying out all the rainbow-colored art pencils. Jake and Pegasus bought matching skull-and-crossbone rainbow badges. Darcy and Star trotted past, wearing feather boas and unicorn-horn headbands,

heading for the elevator to the café. Raheem was showing Brave the books about animal facts. And Flo was squealing with delight at all the cuddly toys.

BRUCE
ANIMAL FACTS
5000
JIGSAW
BRUCE
BRUCE

Mira left Dave at the café having a large hot chocolate (with extra marshmallows) and headed downstairs again to join Flo.

"Mira, I can't decide which kitticorn to get! Do you like the pink one or the lavender one?" Flo was holding up two kitticorn cuddly toys. "OR should I get this life-size lambicorn OR this slothicorn? I just can't decide!"

Mira laughed. "They're all super cool." She reached into a basket of toy chickicorns and rummaged around until she found a pale blue one. She smiled. She knew Dave would love it.

Bruce Hasselhoof appeared at the gift-shop doorway. He looked different. His eyes were a little wild and his hair was standing up all over

the place. Mira wondered if Class Red were more energetic than their usual visitors.

"Who did it?" Bruce cried.

"Who did what?" asked Freya.

"The field . . . my . . . sparklecorn, it's . . . it's all . . . hoof-marks . . . flattened!"

"Bruce, you're not making any sense," said Freya.

Miss Glitterhorn stormed down the stairs from the café. "Who on EARTH flattened the sparklecorn field?" she shouted. "Class Red, this is unacceptable."

Miss Glitterhorn did *not* look relaxed anymore. Mira gulped. They'd only flattened one square yard, she thought. Although they had trotted back and forth through the sparklecorn several times . . .

"Hey! We made a maze!" Darcy yelled from upstairs.

Everyone looked up at Darcy on the café balcony. She waved at them to join her. Bruce Hasselhoof took the stairs two at a time. Class Red followed a little more slowly. Miss Glitterhorn looked at the elevator, but it was full of unicorns, so she climbed the stairs, too. Soon everyone was on the café balcony, looking out at the flattened sparklecorn field.

Mira's throat felt dry. They had flattened a LOT more corn than she realized.

Bruce cleared his throat. "This is unbelievable."

Miss Glitterhorn put her hands on her hips. "Darcy, Mira, Raheem, and Jake. What *have*

you been doing? Have you damaged BARCC property? If I find that you ran away from Bruce's carefully planned awesome activities, then there will be consequences! As Bruce said, that sort of behavior is totally unacceptable!"

"No, no," said Bruce faintly. "I said it was un*believable*. Not unacceptable. There was a maze here back when I completed the quest, but it got overgrown. I've wanted another one ever since."

"So for a million years," said Darcy.

Bruce ignored Darcy. "Mazes are *amazing*!" he said in delight.

Miss Glitterhorn didn't know what to say, so Darcy quickly started three cheers for the new maze before she could stop them.

Raheem rummaged in his backpack. He pulled out the quest checklist and cleared his throat.

"Um, Mr. Hasselhoof? I think we've sort of completed the quest."

The rest of Class Red gasped. Bruce and Miss Glitterhorn hurried over and looked at their checklist. Raheem explained how they'd found the answers to the first four riddles.

"And then, number five is 'What is an amazing sight inside which you cannot see,'" he continued. "Well, you just said that our maze in the sparklecorn field is 'amazing' and we couldn't see it when we were inside it."

"Wonderful work!" Bruce was ecstatic. "That question must be left over from when we had the old maze. No wonder no one ever completed the quest. But you DID!" His face

fell. "Oh, but there are no quest medals. No one's completed it for so long that we just stopped keeping them in stock."

Darcy gave Mira a nudge. "I'm sorry, Mira. I know you love medals."

Mira hugged her friend. "You know what?" she said. "Today was so awesome. It doesn't need a medal."

"NO, WAIT!" Bruce dashed off. He came back a minute later holding a boot from the boot station with *BARCC Medal* written on it in mud. "You can take this as a trophy of your excellence."

Jake snatched it away from Bruce before anyone else could get their hands on it. "As unofficial

Field Trip

quest leader, I think I deserve to keep this," he said.

Dave trotted up and nibbled the toe off the boot so now it said, *BARCC Me*.

Mira, Raheem, and Darcy burst into laughter. They high-fived Jake and he joined in with the laughter, too.

Bruce clapped his hands. "Right-o, kids, time to get rid of you! Ha ha, only joking. But seriously, get on the bus."

Class Red scrambled to buy their souvenirs and then lined up outside the bus. Miss Glitterhorn was collecting clipboards and ticking the children's names off her list as they got on board.

"Raheem, Seb, Freya, Flo—hang on, Flo,

what's that on your back?" Miss Glitterhorn said, stopping Flo.

"What's what?" said Flo, turning around in circles to look behind her. Mira saw that Flo was wearing a cute, furry, slothicorn backpack.

"I didn't see any of those backpacks for sale in the shop. Where were they? Can I go back and get one?" demanded Darcy.

Bruce Hasselhoof let out a yelp. "That's not a backpack, it's a real slothicorn! What did I say the first rule of BARCC was, everyone?"

"Stay where I can see you at all times," said Raheem.

"Ah. But the MOST important rule is DO NOT take the baby animals home!" said Bruce.

"Oopsie!" said Flo. "I didn't realize we were still cuddling. He must have fallen asleep on me. Here you go."

She carefully peeled the slothicorn off her back and handed him to Bruce. The slothicorn stirred but quickly fell asleep again and started snoring on Bruce's shoulder.

As the Rainbow Bus pulled away from BARCC and started making its way back to Unicorn School, Mira went to sit next to Jake.

"Thanks for all your help today, Jake," she said.

Jake grinned. "I guess it *was* kind of cool meeting the kitticorns."

Mira reached into her gift-shop bag and pulled out a small cuddly toy kitticorn. She handed it to Jake. "Sorry they didn't have a golden one."

Jake's eyes got really wide. "Is that really for me?"

Mira nodded. Jake took the kitticorn toy from her tentatively.

"No one's ever given me a present at Unicorn School before," he said.

Mira smiled as Jake cradled the toy in his arms.

"I mean, obviously I get presents all the time at home," he added quickly.

"Okay," said Mira.

Then Jake leaned into Pegasus and fell asleep.

Dave was snoring softly next to Mira. She pulled the blue chickicorn toy out of her bag and tucked it into Dave's mane, so it would always remind him of the cute and cuddly chickicorn that he'd looked after so well.

Then Mira looked around the bus at all her classmates dozing, snuggled up to their unicorns. They'd learned a lot at BARCC. They'd learned about the importance of soil and sparklecorn. They'd learned that goaticorns eat, well, everything, and how not to take a slothicorn home with you. But they'd also learned that shiny medals weren't the be-all and end-all. What really mattered was having an awesome time with your friends and taking care of each other. With the added bonus of being able to brag to Rani when she got home about winning a quest!

All Mira had wanted this morning was a kitticorn cuddle. But the most important thing she'd learned today was something she'd always known, deep down. That cuddles from her UBFF were the very best of all.

Mira snuggled into Dave, who gave a sleepy fart. And a moment later she was fast asleep, too.

WHICH ANIMAL-ICORN ARE YOU?

1. *Would you rather have a cozy film night at home or go out to the movies?*
   a. Movies at home, please! My sofa is so comfy. I'll make the popcorn.
   b. I would rather sleep.
   c. Let's go out! The movies are so exciting.
   d. I don't mind, as long as there are snacks. Did you say doughnuts?

2. *Would you rather live in a forest or a shed?*
   a. A nice, warm shed, please. With lots of rainbow straw.
   b. I don't mind, I can sleep anywhere.
   c. Ooh, the forest would be awesome!
   d. The shed, as long as there are snacks there.

3. *At school, would you rather be amazing at music or science?*
   a. Music—to accompany my friends in a sing-along.
   b. Music sends me to sleeeeeeeep.
   c. Science is super cool.
   d. Science, so I could invent new snacks.

4. *Would you rather play sports or chess?*
   a. Chess—I like indoor games.
   b. I'm too sleepy for games.

c. Sports! Let's go!
d. Is it chocolate sports or chocolate chess?

5. *For your birthday, would you rather have a crafts or trampolining party?*
a. Crafts—I like making pom-poms.
b. Zzzzzzzz.
c. Trampolining—woohoo!
d. Just the cake for me, thanks.

6. *If you were a superhero, would you rather be invisible or be able to fly?*
a. Invisible. Chickens can't fly.
b. Invissizzzzzzz.
c. Fly! That would be awesome!
d. I would like to be invisible and be able to fly to find the best snacks.

Answers

Mostly As: You're a chickicorn! Sweet and fluffy, you know there's no place like home!

Mostly Bs: You're a slothicorn! You're—yawn—just—yawn—soooo sleepy zzzzz.

Mostly Cs: You're a kitticorn! Cute and playful, you're always full of energy.

Mostly Ds: You're Dave the unicorn! You love snacks and getting your own way, but you're always there for your friends.

UNICORN JOKES

What do you call a cold unicorn?
A blue-nicorn.

What do you call a scary unicorn?
A boo-nicorn.

What do you call a unicorn with a candy stuck in its teeth?
A chew-nicorn.

What do you call a unicorn trying to solve a mystery?
A clue-nicorn.

What do you call a unicorn that's bigger in the mornings?
A grew-nicorn.

What do you call an artistic unicorn?
A drew-nicorn.

What do you call a lady sheep with a horn on her head?
A ewe-nicorn.

What do you call a unicorn with the sniffles?
A flu-nicorn.

What do you call a unicorn on safari?
A gnu-nicorn.

What do you call a unicorn running to the bathroom?
A needs-to-poop-icorn.

What do you call a relieved unicorn?
A phew!-nicorn.

Wonder how Dave and Mira's story began?
If you missed it, everybody's favorite
unicorn best friends first met in
Dave the Unicorn: Welcome to Unicorn School!

Turn the page for a sneak peek!

JULY
SALE
50%

CHAPTER ONE
Magic Monday

It was Monday morning and Mira Desai was VERY excited. This was no ordinary Monday morning. This Monday morning was the first day of summer vacation AND it was Mira's first day at a new school! Because this was no ordinary school . . . this was:

UNICORN SCHOOL!

Mira had been desperate to go to Unicorn School since her sister, Rani, started going two summers ago. Rani wouldn't stop going on about how wonderful her unicorn, Angelica, was. She kept saying how *amazing* she was at all the magical quests. And she was always making whinnying noises in Mira's ear to make her jealous. AND she'd brought home about a hundred Unicorn School quest medals, which had their own special shelf in the living room.

Rani said that quests could go on for days and days and were super exciting. And the time Rani spent at Unicorn School did seem *endless* to Mira. But time passed differently at Unicorn School, and Rani was really only ever gone for a day in normal time.

Mira had dreamed of having her own unicorn since FOREVER. She practiced braiding the manes and tails of all her toy horses, persuaded her dad to let her groom his beard, and even tried attaching a horn to their cat, Pickles. He wasn't very pleased.

It was a bit of a mystery who was selected to go to Unicorn School and who wasn't. Lots of people from Mira's family *had* gone to Unicorn School, including Mira's mom, so Mira had hoped more than anything that she would get to go, too. Mira always tried to live her life as open to magic as possible. She wished on stars, she believed in fairies, she said hello to black cats who crossed her path. And then, one incredible day, Mira had woken up with a sparkly envelope on her pillow.

Mira remembered it as if it were yesterday. (It was actually last Thursday.) She screamed so loudly that Pickles flung himself off Mira's bed into a pile of dirty clothes, and Mira's dad came running in to check what was wrong.

But there was nothing wrong. Everything was finally right. Her hands shaking with excitement, Mira opened the letter.

Dear Mira Desai,

We are delighted to invite you to join us at Unicorn School. You will be in Class RED.

Please use the Magic Portal to access the school. We look forward to seeing you soon.

Yours sincerely,
Madame Shetland

"DAD!" Mira yelled, and started jumping on the bed. "I'M GOING TO UNICORN SCHOOL!"

Terrified, Pickles jumped onto Mira's dad's face and wouldn't let go of his beard. "Mfmfmfmf!" he said cheerfully, and gave Mira a thumbs-up before leaving the room and walking into the wall.

Mira reached inside the envelope and pulled out a leaflet containing all the information about the school, including a map and the School Rules. Mira thought she might faint with delight. Unicorn School was going to be AMAZING!

For one thing, Mira couldn't WAIT to bring home her own medals. She'd already started making a space for them on the shelf (and had *accidentally* knocked a couple of Rani's medals into Pickles's bowl).

But the thing Mira was MOST excited about was getting to meet her unicorn.

Her sister said that the unicorns were *specially* chosen for each person for specific magical reasons. You would get to spend all day every day with your unicorn: going to lessons, working on projects, and going on quests. Basically your unicorn would be your best friend.

Mira had a best friend already at normal school (Katie with a *K*), but she could definitely squeeze another one into her life. She'd spent a lot of time thinking about her dream unicorn best friend (Princess Delilah Sparklehoof). She'd filled a whole notebook with drawings of her and made a list of all the incredible things they would do together.

UBFs 4 EVER

1. Have amazing, magical adventures!

2. Be great at quests

3. Get TONS OF MEDALS

#1

Before heading to the Magic Portal that would take them to Unicorn School, Mira's mom took them to the supermarket. Mira and Rani needed to get treats for their unicorns, and Mom needed to buy doughnuts for someone's birthday at work.

Mira wondered what treats unicorns liked.

Which aisle do you go to for magic treats? she thought to herself. But when she asked her sister, Rani rolled her eyes and said, "Unicorns like carrots, *obviously.*" And so they all headed over to the vegetable aisle.

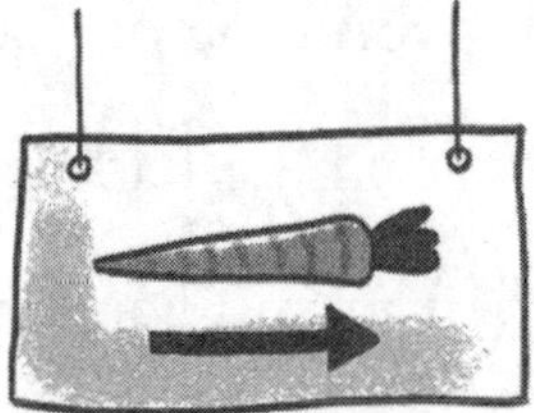

When they'd bought their carrots, they went back to the car. Rani also had some hay left over from last semester and Mom thought it would be nice if she shared it with Mira.

The Magic Portal was in the parking lot by the rec center. Mira had never actually seen it—the portal could only be seen by current Unicorn School students. Even Mira's mom couldn't see it anymore, since she had left Unicorn School roughly a thousand years ago. Usually when they dropped her off, Rani got out around the corner so that she wouldn't be seen with them. But TODAY Mira would be going with her. And she would be one step closer to meeting her unicorn!

There had been quite a bit of traffic on the way and Mom was running late for work.

"It's okay, Mom," said Rani. "I'll take Mira through."

Mom looked from one sister to the other and then at her watch.

"Fine," she said. And then she fixed Rani with a LOOK. "Make sure you take care of your little sister on her first day."

Mom handed them their treat bags, gave them

both a hug, and jumped back in the car. Rani had already started stomping off when Mom rolled down her window. She leaned out with her phone in hand.

"Girls! Let me take a picture. It's your first day at Unicorn School together!"

Rani turned, groaned, and folded her arms. "MOM, are you crying? That's so embarrassing."

Mom sniffed. "It brings back such amazing memories of MY first day at Unicorn School! Oh, happy times . . ." Their mom stared off into the distance for a moment, then she smiled and blew her nose. "Now, smile girls!"

Rani rolled her eyes. Mira smiled and gave two thumbs up as Mom's phone camera **CLICKED**.

That's all we have room for,
but you can catch up on all of Mira
and Dave's adventures at Unicorn School
in the below books!

DIARY
UBFs 4 EVER
PUPIL